Enid Blyton's

Here Comes
NODDY
Again!

Illustrated by Peter Longden

Macdonald Purnell

0 361 07178 7
Text copyright © 1986 Darrell Waters Limited
Illustrations copyright © 1986 Macdonald and Co
(Publishers) Limited
This edition first published 1986 by Purnell Books
a division of Macdonald and Co (Publishers) Limited
Greater London House
Hampstead Road
London NW1 7QX
a BPCC plc company
Made and printed in Great Britain

British Library Cataloguing in Publication Data
Blyton, Enid
  Here comes Noddy Again.–(Noddy library; 4)
  I. Title   II. Series
  823′.912[J] PZ7

Everyone in Toyland knew little Noddy and his red and yellow car. They all waved at him in the streets.

"Parp-parp!" went the horn as they drove around and about Toyland, taking toys here, there and everywhere.

Noddy did his job so well that he became a very busy taxi-driver. He was so friendly and polite that everyone liked him. He sometimes gave the tiny insects free rides and he always picked up the clockwork mouse when he saw him hurrying to catch the toy train. One morning there was a loud knock at Noddy's smart green front door.

"Noddy! Will you take me to the Village of Bouncing Balls?"

Noddy opened the door. The clockwork clown was

outside rolling head-over-heels on the lawn. Someone had used his key to wind him up and set him going.

"Do stop, clown," said Noddy. "You make me feel so dizzy! Look, you've squashed one of my plants. Whatever do you want to go to the Village of Bouncing Balls for, anyway?"

"I want to find a ball to help me in my circus act," said the clown. "I plan to do a new trick with it."

Noddy drove his car out of the garage and the clown jumped in.

"Will you sit still for a minute!" said Noddy. "If you don't I'll probably run into a lamp-post."

"All right," said the clown mischievously. "Though I would rather like to see you knock a lamp-post down ker-runch! What a noise it would make."

"Now you're being silly," said Noddy, as they drove away. At last they arrived at the Village of Bouncing Balls.

"Wait for me, Noddy!" said the clown, when he saw some balls bouncing in the distance. "I'll go and find a really nice ball."

The clown got out of the car and rolled away, head over heels, as fast as ever he could. It wasn't long before a big ball bounced up to Noddy's car and started bouncing around merrily.

"Please don't do that," said Noddy politely. "You might accidentally bounce on to my car and squash it flat, and me too!"

When another ball arrived and joined in the bouncing Noddy began to get worried and drove off towards a rabbit hole. He would be safe there. But the balls bounced after him. Noddy was so worried that he really didn't see where he was going. He ran into two other

NOD 1

balls who were bouncing in the middle of the road.

"Whoooooosshh!" hissed one of the balls and Noddy gazed in dismay at a big dent he had made in it. There was a hole there, and a loud wssssshhhh-ing noise as the air blew out.

Before Noddy could apologise, all kinds of brightly coloured balls came bouncing out from the woods and surrounded the little red and yellow car. Then the clockwork clown came hurrying up, too, with a little ball bouncing beside him.

"Now what have you done, Noddy?" he said. "Dented a ball? How careless of you! My word how angry these balls look. Come on we'd better be going!"

Noddy drove away at top speed with all the balls doing their best to bounce on top of the car. Noddy zigzagged all the way down the woodland path trying to avoid the angry balls till at last he was out of the Village of Bouncing Balls.

Only one ball was left bouncing merrily behind the car.

"Don't worry about that one," said the clown. "It's the one I've asked to come and help me at the circus. I think it likes us, it's following us like a dog."

So it did. Bouncity-bouncity-bounce, all the way to the friendly streets of Toy Town.

"I don't think I want to go to the Village of Bouncing Balls again," said Noddy. "It's too dangerous!"

The clown laughed and jumped out of the car. The little ball rolled up beside him.

"No more bouncing please," said the clown. "I want to practise walking on you, and see if we can do that circus trick I taught you," said the clown. He balanced cleverly on top of the ball as it rolled along and away down the street they went.

One day Noddy got a message from Mr Straw, the farmer at the toy farm, which said:

'Please will you be so kind as to collect some of my hens and ducks and take them to market for me?'

"Well, it will make a change to take hens and ducks in my car instead of toys," laughed Noddy. "I hope they'll be good."

Noddy liked the farm very much. It had a big duck pond, a pink barn, sheds, fences and all sorts of animals. He drove up to the farm-house door and hooted his horn. Mrs Straw opened the door and smiled when she saw who it was.

"Oh hello Noddy," she said.

"Mr Straw has the hens and ducks ready for you at the hen house. You can take a short cut across the fields to get there. But do be careful!"

Noddy drove slowly across the bumpy fields and carefully closed all the gates behind him so that the animals wouldn't get out. In one of the fields, Noddy met a goat who didn't like visitors. It ran at the little red and yellow car and butted it hard. The little car flew up into the air and turned over! Noddy fell out onto a hedge and the car splashed into the duck pond. When the farmer came out of the hen house to see what the noise was he couldn't believe his eyes.

"Do you usually drive your car over hedges Noddy?" he laughed.

"It was your goat's fault!" said Noddy crossly. "Come and help me down, Mr Straw. I'm stuck in

your hedge. It's a good job my body is wooden!"

Mr Straw fetched a ladder and helped Noddy down from the hedge, then they went to look at the car. Noddy and the farmer tried to pull it out of the duck pond but they couldn't. It was firmly stuck upside down in the water.

"We'll have to empty the pond," said Noddy. "It's the only way we'll get it out." Mr Straw called to his farm animals. "Buttercup, Daisy, Woolly, Long-Ears, come here, all of you!"

All the cows, donkeys, sheep and pigs collected round the pond to look at Noddy's car upside down in the pond.

"Now drink," said Mr Straw to all his animals. "Drink as much water as you can. Quickly now!"

Daisy, Buttercup, Woolly and all the other toy farm animals drank as much as they could.

The water level sank lower and lower until at last the pond was almost empty. The animals stopped drinking, and Mr Straw and Noddy waded into the pond. With much pulling and pushing they turned the little car up the right way. Then they tugged it up onto the bank where Mr and Mrs Straw helped Noddy to dry and polish it. When they had finished the car was shiny again. Even the horn still worked. Parp-parp!

Then it was time to go and the hens and ducks all crowded onto the car seat beside Noddy. They quacked and clucked loudly as they settled down together.

"Here's a shiny new penny for the fare," said Mr Straw. "You can keep any eggs that the hens lay on the way. I'm sorry our goat caused you so much trouble."

And off they went. One of the hens insisted on perching on Noddy's head which made it very difficult for him to drive his little car, but eventually he got to market, where he found Mr Straw's brother and handed over the excited birds.

Would you believe it, when Noddy got back into the car to drive home, there were eleven eggs on the seat beside him! Eleven! Noddy stared at them in delight.

"Eleven eggs for my breakfast!" he chuckled. "What a stroke of good luck!"

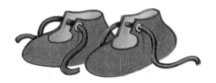

One day a goblin called at Noddy's House-for-One. The goblin didn't knock, instead he poked his head round the door and made Noddy jump. He almost spilt his cup of tea.

"Are you Noddy the taxi-driver?" he asked.

"Yes I am. But please don't peep round the door like that. Come in!" said Noddy. "What do you want?"

"I want to go to a party in the Dark Wood tonight at midnight," said the goblin with a naughty grin.

"Oh, I don't think it's a good idea to go to the Dark Wood in the middle of the night," said Noddy. "It's so very dark there! Big-Ears has told me all about you mischievous goblins."

"Big-Ears? Why, don't take any notice of that old brownie! It'll be great fun, and look, I've got a great big bag of sweets here, fruit drops, your favourite! You can have them all if you take me tonight," said the goblin.

Noddy liked sweets very much. A whole bag of fruit drops. Mmm...it was tempting. He thought about it so much that the bell on his hat jingled a tune.

"All right then," he said at last. "I'll take you. But I warn you, I've done hardly any driving at night and I really don't like the Dark Wood even in the daytime."

"Fiddlesticks," said the goblin, "I'll be with you won't I? You can come to the party, too, if you like. It'll be a lot of fun, and then you can take me back home afterwards. I'll give you another bag of sweets."

Noddy nodded his head madly. Two bags of sweets! All those fruit drops — and just for a drive in the middle of the night.

Who cared about the Dark Wood? Anyway, the moon would be shining, and he wouldn't be all on his own.

Later that night Noddy drove his little car out of the garage. All of a sudden, a voice speaking from the darkness made him jump. It was so dark Noddy couldn't see who was there.

"Are you ready?" it squeaked. The goblin was standing in the shadows. Noddy got out to see where the voice was coming from and when he got out of the car bumped right into him.

"Oh, sorry," he said. "Yes I'm ready. Here is the car. Jump in!"

The goblin chuckled and climbed in. Noddy switched the little car's lights on. They shone out brightly, and as they drove down the streets of Toy Town the goblin began to sing a peculiar song.

"It isn't very good
In the Dark Dark Wood
In the middle of the night
When there isn't any light;
It isn't very good
In the Dark Dark Wood."

"Please don't sing that song," said Noddy. "You're making me nervous. I shall drive into a tree or something, and then we won't be able to go to the party. Be quiet, goblin."

The goblin did stop singing, but he kept making little chuckling noises which Noddy didn't like at all.

"I wish I hadn't come," he thought. "I do wish I hadn't come!"

They arrived at the Dark Wood at the stroke of midnight. The lights of Noddy's little car made bright paths between the trees as they drove along the bumpy lanes.

"Where's this party of yours supposed to be?" asked Noddy. "I don't think I want to drive any deeper into the wood. I'll get lost."

"Well, stop here then," said the goblin and Noddy stopped. Where was the party? And the band? Where were the lights, and happy voices that Noddy expected?

"It's so quiet," Noddy whispered. "Where can everyone be?"

"There isn't going to be a party!" chuckled the goblin nastily. "This is a trap, Noddy, we're after your little car, get out at once!"

Noddy was so frightened that he couldn't move. He couldn't speak either. A trap! Whose trap?

And why did they want his little car?

Then things happened very quickly. Three goblins jumped out from behind a tree and came running towards him. Before Noddy could do anything, they had grabbed him and pulled him right out of his car and threw him on to the ground.

The goblin who had come with him took the wheel.

"What did I tell you?" he laughed loudly. "It isn't very good in the Dark Dark Wood, is it? Come on you lot, let's go."

"Wait a minute," said one of the other goblins. "Noddy's hat's got a jingle bell at the top. I think I'll take it, it would suit me!"

"And I'll have his shoes!" said another as he grabbed Noddy.

They pulled off his hat and shoes and then piled into the little car.

"Hey, give those back!" shouted Noddy bravely, but there were just too many goblins to fight all at once.

"Ha, ha, ho, ho!" laughed the naughty goblins as they drove off at top speed. R-r-r-r-r roared the little red and yellow car. The sound grew fainter and fainter, until at last Noddy couldn't hear it any more and suddenly everything was quiet.

Noddy was alone in the Dark Wood. The cold wind whistled and he remembered the goblin's song "It isn't very good in the Dark Dark Wood," and he stood up, trembling.

"Help!" he shouted. "Help! I'm lost!"

Noddy shook with fear as he stumbled through the bushes into a moonlit clearing. There before him was a toadstool house. Noddy jumped for joy, ran over to it and banged at the door. Big-Ears the brownie put his head out of the window and stared in surprise at the little nodding figure down below.

"Noddy! Is it you? What are you doing out here in the middle of the night with your hat and shoes missing? Am I dreaming?"

"No you're not dreaming Big-Ears! Let me in! I'm cold!"

Big-Ears ran downstairs and unlocked the heavy wooden door of his toadstool house and soon he was listening to Noddy's story as they both sat by a blazing fire.

"You told me never to take
sweets from strangers, and you
were right," sighed Noddy. "Those
goblins stole my car and my shoes,
even my little hat with a bell on it!
Oh, I'm so unhappy. I wish I could get my hands on them
…Whooss-shooo!" he sneezed.

"What a loud sneeze!" said Big-Ears. "You must go home to
bed or you'll catch a dreadful chill. I'll lend you some clothes."

So, wearing one of Big-Ears' coats, a scarf and some slippers,
Noddy hurried with his friend through the Dark Wood to Toy
Town. When they got there they woke up Mr Plod the
policeman, and he was most astonished to hear their tale.

"Ah-whoo-shoo!" sneezed Noddy again as Big-Ears hurried
him away to his House-for-One. Noddy waved goodbye to

Big-Ears, locked the front door, went straight to bed with two hot water bottles and fell fast asleep.

In the morning Noddy was woken up by a tapping on his door. It was Big-Ears bringing him some breakfast.

"Now you stay in bed today and nurse your cold," beamed Big-Ears kindly. "Don't worry about anything. I know how to get your car back and when you're better I'll tell you all about my plan. After all that is what friends are for."

The news that Noddy was ill and had been robbed soon travelled around Toy Town. People were knocking on the door all day long!

"Can I come in?" Mrs Tubby

called. "I've brought you some fruit."

Mr Straw came with some eggs and the clockwork clown brought flowers.

"What a lot of kind friends I have!" laughed Noddy.

When everyone had gone back to their homes, Big-Ears showed Noddy a large notice he had made. It read:

'WILL ANYONE WHO HEARS A BELL JINGLING PLEASE TELL BIG-EARS'

Not half an hour after Big-Ears had pinned the notice to the door of Noddy's House-for-One, a clockwork mouse knocked at the door and came in.

"Please Mr Big-Ears I've heard a bell jingling inside an old hollow tree at the edge of the Dark Wood, near the stream," he whispered.

"Have you?" chuckled Big-Ears.

"That is just what I wanted to know. Now we know that those bad goblins are hiding in the old hollow tree. I'll go there with Mr Plod at once! There's no time to lose."

Noddy was so excited that his head nodded twice as fast as he lay in bed waiting for the next bit of news about his car and clothes.

Mr Plod and Big-Ears called on Mr Straw and asked him if they could borrow one of his big sacks. Then they visited the clockwork clown and asked him to bring along his ball. Together, they set off.

It wasn't long before they were standing on the edge of the Dark Wood near to a hollow tree.

"Ssh!" said Big-Ears. "I can hear those naughty goblins laughing inside the tree. Do you remember the plan?" The others nodded. "Right then let's go!"

The clown whispered some-
thing to the bouncy ball and
bouncity-bounce it bounced right
into the clearing. Then with a
mighty jump it bounced right into
the hollow tree. There were squealing and scrabbling noises
from inside the tree as the goblins tried to scramble out from
the hole.

When they did, Big-Ears, Mr Plod and the clockwork clown
were there holding the big sack. Plop! One goblin jumped out
of the hollow tree into the sack. Plonk, plonk! That was another
two. Clunk! That was the last one and the biggest one of all.

"Got 'em!" shouted Big-Ears as Mr Plod tied up the neck of
the sack tightly so that none could escape.

"Let's find Noddy's car!" said the clockwork clown and he

rolled head over heels into the hole at the bottom of the hollow tree. Sure enough, there was Noddy's little car.

"Put the sack of goblins into the car and I'll drive them back to the police station straight away," said Mr Plod.

"I'll follow behind on my bicycle," said Big-Ears.

"And I'll roll after you on my clever ball!" chuckled the clockwork clown turning head over heels.

What a sight they all made, as they set off through the Dark Wood with their sack of goblins.

When they arrived in Toyland they stopped outside Noddy's House-for-One. The policeman hooted the horn of the little red and yellow car. Parp-parp! Parp-parp! Big Ears rang his bicycle bell loudly.

Noddy jumped out of bed at once and came to the window.

"Hello, there!" shouted Big-Ears. "We've got your car back for you!"

"And as soon as I've delivered this bag of goblins to the police station, you'll have your hat and

shoes as well!" shouted Mr Plod.

"Hurry back, and bring a big cake, Big-Ears. I feel well again and I'm going to have a party to celebrate!"

And that's just what they did. Mr Plod brought the goblins along to say they were sorry. Big-Ears made them polish the little red and yellow car until it shone like new.

The clockwork clown and his bouncing ball put on a special show for the guests at Noddy's party. Noddy's hat jingled merrily as he welcomed his guests.

"How lucky I am to have so many good friends," he smiled.

"How lucky Toyland is to have such a good taxi-driver!" laughed Mr Straw.

"What a good idea it was to invite Mr Straw's ducks and hens," laughed Big-Ears. "Now we can all have eggs for tea!"